SPIDER'S BABY-SITTING JOB

by Robert Kraus

SCHOLASTIC INC.

New York Toronto London Auckland Sydney

ISBN 0-590-42445-9

12 11 10 9 8 7 6 5 4 3 2 1   0 1 2 3 4 5/9

Printed in the U.S.A.   23

First Scholastic printing, September 1990

I had just straightened up my room and I was feeling pretty good when the telephone rang.

It was Ladybug. "Fly and I are baby-sitting for the Bedbugs, and things are getting out of hand," she cried. "Can you come right over?"

I dropped everything and ran over at top speed.
Ladybug was in trouble, and trouble is my business.

There were a lot of yells and screams coming from the Bedbug house. What could be going on?

I pushed open the front door. I couldn't believe my eyes! The Bedbugs were biting Ladybug and Fly was all tied up.

"Help!" cried Ladybug.
"Don't worry, Spider's here," I replied.
I shooed the Bedbugs away from Ladybug and
untied Fly.

I'd never been a baby-sitter before, but I *had* been
a baby.
I knew I could make those Bedbugs go to sleep.

I took the baby Bedbugs out for a walk to tire
them out.
They didn't get tired—but I did. Puff, puff.

I made them a snack.
Mmm—tasted pretty good.

"It's story time!" I said.
"Goody!" screamed the Bedbugs.
I read them my favorite bug books.
I started nodding off, but they didn't.

I gave them a bath.
We all got wet.
"We won't go to bed 'til Mommy and Daddy come home!" they cried.

That would never do.
They had to be in bed before Mr. and Mrs. Bedbug
came home.
And that was any minute!
Then I got a great idea.

I dressed Fly and Ladybug up as
Mr. and Mrs. Bedbug.

"Mommy and Daddy are home!" I shouted.
"Who are you kidding?" said Brucie Bedbug. "That's
not Mommy and Daddy, that's Fly and Ladybug!"

They were right. What could I say?
The baby Bedbugs were playing Slug-a-Bug and
Bedbug Bingo. They just wouldn't go to bed.

Then I got another idea. I started yawning and yawning and yawning.
It wasn't hard to do.

"Do as I do," I whispered to Fly and Ladybug.
Fly and Ladybug started yawning and yawning.
Fly even fell asleep.

Suddenly all the little Bedbugs began yawning and yawning and yawning.

"Please let us go to bed, Spider," cried little Beverly Lou Bedbug.

"No way," I said. I gave Ladybug a big wink.

"We want to go to sleep! We want to go to sleep!"
cried all the little Bedbugs.

"Well...okay—since you insist," I said.
And they brushed their teeth and popped into
bed quicker than you could say "pajamas."

Just then Mr. and Mrs. Bedbug came home.
"How are my little angels?" asked Mrs. Bedbug.

"Fast asleep and snug as a bug," said Ladybug.
"I hope they weren't too much trouble," said
Mr. Bedbug, giving Ladybug three cents.
"Thank you," said Ladybug, "and now we must
be going."

"The three of us did it together," I said.
"The three baby-sitters."
"Goodnight," I said. "Hope the bedbugs don't bite."
And we laughed all the way home.

The End